MW01247311

Beautiful Don

Kathryn May Howard Whitaker

Kathryn Whitaker

PAGE PUBLISHING, INC.
New York, NY

First originally published by Page Publishing, Inc. 2018

Written and Illustrated by
Kathryn May Howard Whitaker © 1982
And a lot of help from Jerry Whitaker

ISBN 978-1-64298-035-6 (Hardcover)
ISBN 978-1-64298-034-9 (Digital)

Printed in the United States of America

This true story is dedicated
to my favorite geese:
Don, Juliet, Gandalf,
and last but not least, Quinine
Thank you Samuel B. Rice, the veterinary, for your
bravery and dedication with keeping Don alive.

SPECIAL THANKS TO

Al Bradford for his editorial help
Marilyn Almguist for narration
Karen Maloney for the music

Bright sunlight is shining as I peek out of the hive that I share with other bees. I'm ready for the new day and a new story. You see, I'm called Thaddeus the storyteller. While other bees gather honey, I collect stories. This story is about Don the white goose.

Mr. Nibs stood on his front porch with his old dog Bo in Carver, Massachusetts. Together they watched Don, a gosling Mr. Nibs adopted, stumbling over tallgrass.

Only to be confronted by a giant plastic flowerpot that looked like a large white goose. Don opened his little wings, flapping them. "Cheep, cheep," he called to the plastic flowerpot. It *was* love at first sight. Don found his mom.

Don grew, changing into a beautiful snowy-white goose, never straying too far from his plastic mother goose!

The afternoon sun warmed the old dog. Maybe Bo had a terrible dream—we'll never know! But Don moved closer to the sleeping dog, munching on tender grass. Quick as an attacking dog could go, Bo snapped out, biting Don on top of his wing. Don went down.

tartled by Bo's attack on Don, Mr. Nibs came running.

"Don!" he shouted, but Don's dark eyes were already closed.

"Oh, Bo, what have you done?"

With gentle hands, Mr. Nibs lifted Don, cradling him in his arms. Too stunned, Don just lay there.

"Oh, Don, your poor wing."

With his wounded wing snug in a bandage that was wrapped around his whole body, Don began the long process of healing. Every day, he nuzzled up to his plastic mother goose.

Mr. Nibs spoke softly to the white goose, "Let me remove your bandage."

Don stood perfectly still as Mr. Nibs cut away the only thing that held his wing in place. Because—alas!—Don's poor wing hung down, tip touching the ground.

As time went on, Mr. Nibs realized Don needed companionship of other geese. He was fondly ruffling his old dog's ears as he thought of this!

"Bo, I know we love Don, but he needs to be with other geese. I've spoken with some friends who have three other geese. They said Don is welcome."

Later that afternoon, Don was placed in the truck. As the old truck bounced down the road, Don's heart began to beat faster.

He peeked out of his box as the old truck rolled to a stop.

Is this my new home? he wondered. *Other geese,* he noticed curiously and became a little frightened.

As the truck pulled away, Don saw it get smaller and smaller, and he wondered where Mr. Nibs was going without him?

And where is my mother goose?

Then two geese dropped their heads with their neck stretched out as far as they could go and ran straight at him.

Don jumped back away from the snapping, pinching beaks. But his foot got caught in his wing, and he somersaulted, going head over heels.

After a flip-flop landing, Don straightened his ruffled feathers and moved back while two gray ganders stopped in amazement. They had never seen anything like that before. The two ganders stocked off, muttering to each other.

"Ah, caterpillar! Have you seen Don?" I asked.

"Yes," the caterpillar said, nodding and munching around a mouthful of oak leaf.

"Where is he now?" I remembered I was speaking to a caterpillar.

"I don't know, but you might ask Bo."

Thaddeus flew to Bo. "Do you know where Don is?"

Bo laid his head down. "Mr. Nibs took Don to be with other geese!"

"Do you know where?"

But Bo did not know.

"Thank you," I offered, flying in the direction of the open field, hoping to see some of my friends along the way who knew where the other geese lived.

*O*h my, I forgot Don's mother goose. I wonder if he is missing the
plastic flowerpot? I wondered.

"Mrs. Rabbit, forgive me for disturbing you, but Mr. Nibs has taken Don. I must find him."

"Calm yourself, Thaddeus. Follow me. We'll show you to the maple tree. From there, your goal is straight ahead to where the geese live. Come, children."

After Mrs. Rabbit left me at the maple tree, I had no problem finding all the geese. I reached there just in time to see Mr. Nibs putting Mother Goose down.

Honking loudly, Don called out to Mother Goose. If not for his wounded wing, he'd have flown to her side.

"My friend," I said, trying to catch my breath.

Don looked up. "Thaddeus, I didn't think I was ever going to see you again. I'm so glad you're here!"

It was an ongoing battle with Don the loser. He tried to defend himself, but his wounded wing got in the way, hanging even lower, dragging the ground constantly.

Every day had its ups and downs, but the downs far outweighed the ups. The two ganders, Guinny and Ganduff, had to be shooed away from Don regularly. Something had to be done.

So an appointment was made with the local veterinarian. The day finally came when Don was taken to see Dr. Sam. Being a curious goose, Don nipped at the shiny stethoscope. Dr. Sam smiled as he examined his wounded wing.

"Don will never be able to use his wing, and in this condition, it can cause more damage. It can serve no purpose except to trip him."

The decision was made. Dr. Sam medicated Don so it would not hurt and removed the wing that would never truly heal. After his operation, Don spent the night.

Just the next day, Don came home, and he felt strong. He was set down on the grass. The other geese, even the birds and squirrels, stilled as they waited to see.

Then Don's chest swelled with a mighty honk, greeting all.

"I'm fine," he called. And indeed, he was.

Juliet, the third goose of the trio, was pleasant in a shy way. She never joined her two crazy brothers Ganduff and Guinny when they chased Don. She told them they were being mean, but they never listened.

Don watched her as she came closer to him.

"So glad you're home, Don," she said sweetly.

"Thank you, Juliet. Me too."

"Would you like to walk with me?" she asked while gazing into his eyes.

Don could hardly reply with the lump he felt in his throat. "Yes, I would love to," Don managed. And together, they walked away.

As I looked over, I was sure Mother Goose was smiling.

With all of his strength back, no longer stumbling, Don was quick shrewd and resourceful—and more than willing when Gandduff charged him. With his head lowered, almost touching the ground, Don countered Gandduff. He struck with lightning speed, catching Gandduff off guard, and the other goose went down hard. Don's powerful bill didn't waste any time paying him back, with more than a few good nips.

Looking back over his shoulder, he glared at Guinny's open beak, ready to pinch. Guinny stared back at him in disbelief. He turned away and ran, with Don hot on his heels giving chase.

Then Don stopped; he had made his point. He wasn't a bully. He knew the ganders wouldn't bother him again.

Together, watching the amber colors of fall chill to a winter white, Don and Juliet fell in love. Spring brought upon the urgency to Juliet and Don. Gathering twigs and leaves together, they made a nest. Juliet settled in, with Don watching over her, always by her side.

Soon all the cracked eggs had openings wide enough for small heads to poke through. When all the bits and pieces of shell fell off, the final count was an even dozen.

Well, it turned out Uncles Gandduff and Guinny were a big help keeping track of twelve little goslings, which was a *full-time* job.

Helping the last little gosling snuggle in for the night, Don and Juliet watched as the sun set.

The End

where"s that snake

Short story written by
Ryley Wayne Larry Whitaker
with help from Grandmother Kathryn Whitaker

Illustrations Drawn by
Ryley Wayne Larry Whitaker

About the Illustrator
Ryley Wayne Larry Whitaker.
He is 7 years old.
Lives in Wenatchee Wa.
With his two dogs "Rex" with his
lazier black eye's, and Doodle's,
and with his mom and dad.
His favorite color is blue.

nister slither's

Once upon a time, a young boy who,s names was Ryley had a pet snake named Mister Slithers.

They were in their back yard, when Mister Slithers, thought he smelled a mouse his favorite food! so he slithered, as only a snake can slither right under the house.

ow Ryley was afraid for
Mister Slithers who had gone
underground under his house,
so he wore a frown.

"WHERE ARE YOU MISTER SLITHER

ow Mister slither's was under the dark house, in seconds he found that darned mouse, like lighting jumping out of a bottle, he was just that quick, and ready to strike.

When all of the sudden the fuzzy mouse jumped up high probable hit his little head, but being a grasshopper mouse it was easy to do. Then landed on the bottom of a window sill and stood very very still.

Mister Slither came closer and closer.

The little mouse just couldn't stand the suspense any longer, he was very tense.

So he yelled in a voice very shrill,

"PLESEEEESE don't eat me today" (GULP) "I'm much to thin," with another big, (gulp),

His voice was the biggest mouse voice, Mister Slither's had ever heard.

""if you get me some cheese, i'll be much fatter, you see, i only wish to please."

Now Mister Slither was much to smart for that mouse.

"What a trickster," Hissed 'Mr slither, "i'm much to smart for him, i live in Ryley's house!" HISS".

So Mister Slither coiled back a bit, then Hissed, "Yes little mouse I'll not eat you today, if you find meeeeth some cheese, bring it into my house, and remember I know where you live, I know your house." mister slither's hist.

Because he really wasn't hungry, and he did hear Ryley calling him.

"Beside's when the silly mouse brings the cheese into my house, I'll be able to catch him again, that's so much more fun."

Then he said with his snake mouth opened wide showing off his white shinning teeth.

"Yes please do eat lots of cheese, you are much thin." His Snake tung flicked back and forth in his snakiest grin.

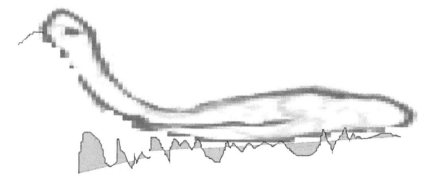

R yley was so happy to see Mister Slither's again,
because he was truly his friend, and he was really
tired of calling him.

The birds were singing, butterflies and bee's were busy collecting pollen.

And Ryley could stop call'en because Mister Slither was home again. And he was just fine.

The End

About the Author

Kathryn May Howard Whitaker was born in Los Angeles, California, on January 20, 1941. Her exceptional talent was evidenced in the fact that she was a self-taught artist and contributed beautiful works of art in numerous genres. In addition to being portrait artist and sculptor, she painted watercolor, oils, pastels, and pen and ink. Mrs. Whitaker could mix any color just by looking at it and would try any medium until she had conquered it. She made her own molds for elves and leaf fairies, and she painted a fresco of the cresol horse. To round out her talent and versatility, she authored and illustrated two (as yet, unpublished) books.

Mrs. Whitaker started the Art Guild in Carver, Massachusetts, in 1979. She succeeded in capturing the charm of, and her love for, New England in her beautiful paintings. She resided in New England for forty-five years and recreated the shorelines of New England from Connecticut to Maine. As a teacher, she shared all her knowledge of the arts with students; she felt strongly that teachers should share all there is to know.

Her work was found in many gift shops and galleries in Plymouth, Massachusetts, and one of her prints of Plymouth Harbor and Wharf is owned by the late Ronald Reagan. As of April 2018, her original oil paintings of *The America's Home Town and Town Wharf-Plymouth Harbor* are now hanging in the 1820 Court House, which is the town hall of Plymouth Massachusetts. These works, and other information, can be found at http://kathrynwhitaker.com/art work prints.html and http://www.legacy.com/orbituaries/wickedlocal-plymouth/obituary.aspx?n=kathryn-whitaker&pid=172756202.

Mrs. Whitaker passed away on October 1, 2014, leaving her astonishing legacy and volume of beautiful works for the world to enjoy.

KATHRYN HOWARD WHITAKER
PORTRAIT ARTIST

Kathryn Whitaker's portraits are a life-creating experience. Drawing from everyday situations like a child would draw from a "wish book". Kathryn has created works of art that become a real part of the lives of those who experience them.

Kathryn chooses as the focal points of her works the "ordinary people", those who normally pass through life unnoticed by the masses. Using this Normal Rockwell technique, she has immortalized those who have touched her life and in doing so, she has touched the lives of many others.

Painting has been a central focus of Kathryn's life for 40 plus years. Her study of people, through their actions, expressions, emotions and ideas, has been a life-long love of hers and has helped her build up a catalog of material from which to draw on her canvas creations.

Kathryn's art education includes formal art courses as well as studying with many artists in the area. Portraitist Craig Cartmell of

Plymouth has shared his knowledge with her as has marine painter Marshall Joyce of Kingston, and also Patty Blanc of Norwell.

Drawing from what she learned from others, along with what she experienced through her own work, Kathryn has grown into the role of teacher. She has opened an art gallery and supply shop in Carver and from there she teaches art to adults and children.

Kathryn's portraits were first offered through Mr. Z's Gallery in Cambridge and the Golden Gull Studio in Plymouth. Today her portraits, many of them commissioned, are seen throughout New England. She also demonstrated a tremendous talent for painting landscapes, seascapes and animals.

This blossoming artist has begun to enter her portraits in art competitions, exhibitions, and shows, including a two-person show in Plymouth's Golden Gull Studio, a one-person show at Kingston Five Cent Savings Bank, and a one-person show at Middleboro Trust Company. Public enthusiasm led to several of her paintings becoming permanent hangings at Plymouth Five Cent Savings and other businesses in that town. Others are displayed at the Marion Art Gallery and Vendo Nubes Gallery in Duxbury.

Kathryn Whitaker, portrait artist, continues to amaze with every new life she sets down on canvas or slate. With the world as her menagerie her gallery of creations shall continue to grow and fascinate those fortunate enough to be drawn to them.

Printed in the USA
CPSIA information can be obtained
at www.ICGtesting.com
LVHW070914101023
760671LV00003B/146